© 1991 Twin Books Corp.

All rights reserved.

This 1991 edition published by Derrydale Books,
distributed by Outlet Book Company, Inc.,
A Random House Company
225 Park Avenue South
New York, NY 10003

Directed by HELENA Productions Ltd.
Illustrated by Van Gool-Lefevre-Loiseaux

Produced by Twin Books
15 Sherwood Place
Greenwich, CT 06830
Printed and bound in Spain

ISBN 0-517-05420-5

8 7 6 5 4 3 2 1

Gulliver's Travels in Lilliput

Van Gool

DERRYDALE BOOKS
New York

Twin Books

Once upon a time, long ago, a young doctor named Gulliver was shipwrecked at sea by a violent storm. Tossed for days on the ocean's waves, with only a slim board to keep him afloat, Gulliver was finally washed ashore on a very strange land.

Exhausted by his ordeal, Gulliver quickly fell into a deep and dreamless sleep. Imagine his surprise, then, when he awakened to find that his arms and legs were strongly fastened to the ground! And his hair, which was long and thick, had been tied down in the same way.

Flat on his back, Gulliver could see only sky. Yet he felt a soft pattering across his body, like the footfalls of a tiny, scurrying army. And he could hear what sounded like a hundred hummingbirds circling round him.

Curious, and not a little frightened, Gulliver struggled to free himself. Finally, he succeeded in gaining the use of his left arm and loosening the bonds on his hair.

Rolling onto his right side, Gulliver was astonished to see a row of six-inch people armed with bows and arrows that were aimed at him!

Unable to speak the language of his captors, Gulliver did his best to signal his friendship and good will to the little people of Lilliput (for it was on the island of Lilliput that Gulliver had landed). The Lilliputians had never seen so large a man before. Although he seemed friendly, and they wanted to trust him, it was decided to take him into the kingdom bound by the ankles. There he could request his liberty from his Imperial Majesty, the Emperor.

With some difficulty, Gulliver got up and bowed deeply to the Emperor, his wife, and the court. His Majesty was impressed by Gulliver's gentle manners.

Welcoming Gulliver to his kingdom, the Emperor ordered two of his greatest scholars to instruct this "Man-Mountain" (as Gulliver was called in Lilliputian) in the language and native customs of Lilliput.

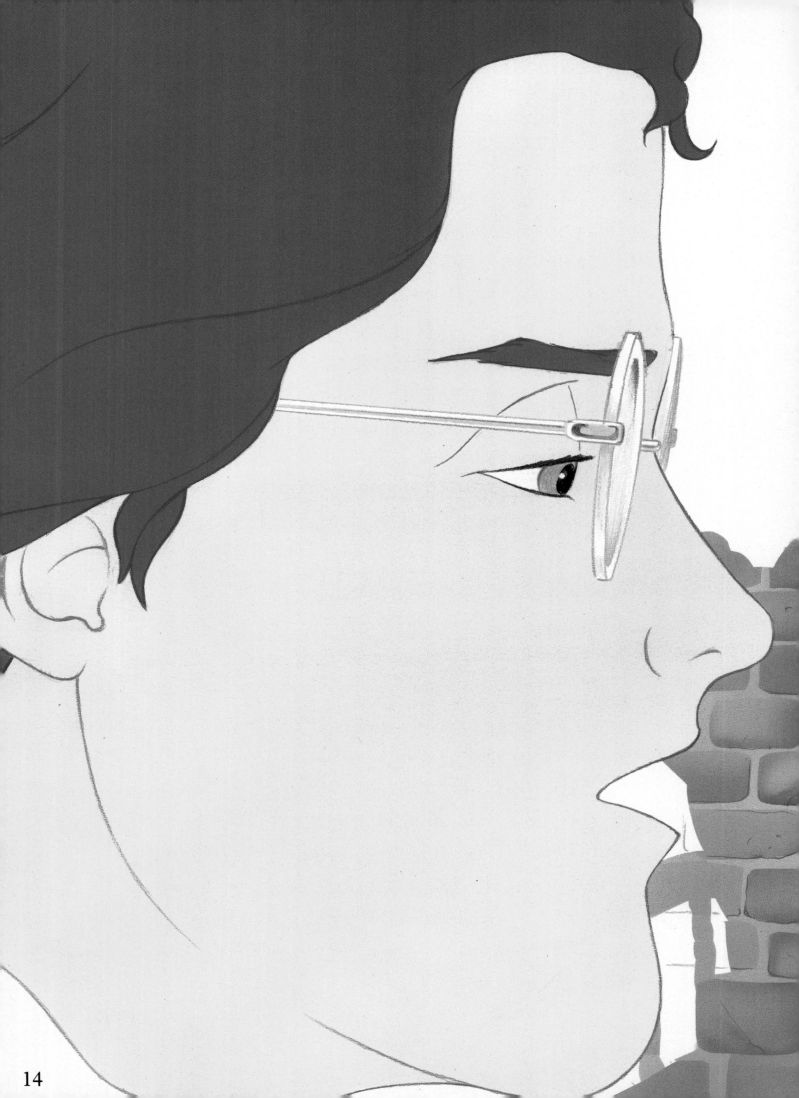

Gulliver had always been a quick learner and had studied many languages at the university. In a short time, he was able to tell the Emperor about his shipwreck. Gulliver promised that no one would be disturbed if he were allowed his freedom among the kind people of Lilliput.

His Majesty listened thoughtfully to Gulliver's request. Then he explained that his guest must be searched before he was released to roam freely around the island.

"Of course," said Gulliver politely.

"Here you are," said the "Man-Mountain," handing over his comb, pocketknife, watch and chain, and a wallet with some gold coins in it.

Now Gulliver had the freedom to explore the island kingdom from shore to shore. And what a fascinating kingdom it was!

One day the Emperor decided to entertain his huge guest with a variety of parades and shows. There were splendid performances by tiny acrobats and athletes. Then the Emperor asked Gulliver to straddle the city's Great Canal like a Colossus, while the royal barge floated beneath!

Gulliver gained the trust and affection of the people of Lilliput so completely that he was presented with a key to the city.

"As a scholar," said the Emperor, "you may wish to study the scrolls that contain the history of Lilliput."

Gulliver was delighted. He spent much time reading these old documents. From them he discovered that the Lilliputians were an ancient and proud people. Their only enemies lived on the island of Blefuscu, across the channel.

Gulliver made friends all over the city. He stopped often on his morning walks to speak to his friend Reldresal, who had breakfast on his balcony so that he could talk to Gulliver over his morning coffee.

No longer were the people of Lilliput afraid of the "Man-Mountain." In fact, it was reassuring to them to see Gulliver towering above the city.

One fine June morning, some months after
Gulliver's arrival, a grand celebration was held
to celebrate the Empress' twenty-sixth
birthday. Gulliver paid his respects to Her
Majesty and renewed his pledge of loyalty.
"Consider me at your service," he said, "in
gratitude for your kindness and generosity."

Not long after this, two excited councilmen from the court came to see Gulliver.

"The Empress has sent us to tell you that we are in danger," they announced. "The Blefuscudians have launched a great fleet of war vessels! Even now, they are sailing across the bay!"

Gulliver set out at once.

Asking the local seamen about the depth of the channel, Gulliver learned that at high tide it was seventy "glumgluffs" deep—about six feet. Quickly, he waded out into the bay. The invaders were so terrified by the sight of this giant that they leaped from their ships and swam back to their own island!

Then Gulliver attached ropes to the prow of each little ship and pulled the entire fleet across the channel to Lilliput!

"Now the foolish wars between these tiny kingdoms will end," he said to himself hopefully.

At the royal port, Gulliver was greeted joyfully by the Emperor and his court. "Long live the most powerful friend of Lilliput!" they cried. Gulliver was honored with the highest title of the land, that of "Nardac."

The Empress directed that a huge display of fireworks be set off in honor of the great day of victory.

But suddenly, another disaster struck! Young Flimnap, the Emperor's favorite nephew, was so excited by the day's events that he shot a firecracker too close to the royal canopy. In seconds, it was aflame! As the people scurried to carry water and stop the spreading fire, Gulliver came to the rescue again. Soaking his handkerchief in water, he squeezed it over the flames and put them out.

Several days later, Gulliver was sitting sadly by the town fountain. He was very homesick, and he did not see how he could ever return to his family and friends. At that moment, a messenger arrived with bad news.

"Another warship from Blefuscu has been sighted on the horizon," he said breathlessly.

"I will go to the harbor," said Gulliver.

Walking to the shore, Gulliver marveled at the fact that Blefuscu was so warlike.

38

He swam over to the other island and spoke to the King of Blefuscu.

"You are wasting your time," he explained. "The Lilliputians call me the Man-Mountain, and they are under my protection. You had better stay at home."

To make sure, he put their last boat in his pocket and returned to Lilliput.

Delighted as he was to have established peace, Gulliver could no longer disguise the fact that he was homesick. Two of the councilmen noticed his sad look and asked him, "What is wrong?"

"I miss my family and friends in England," Gulliver explained. Then he took the tiny Blefuscudian boat from his pocket and asked, "Would the Emperor let you build a boat scaled to my size, to carry me home?"

Of course, the Emperor couldn't refuse so sincere a request by his country's hero. In two weeks the boat was completed and a grand festival held to bid Gulliver farewell. He set off at high noon, waving to all his friends. As he pulled away from shore, colorful balloons rose high above the cheering Lilliputians.

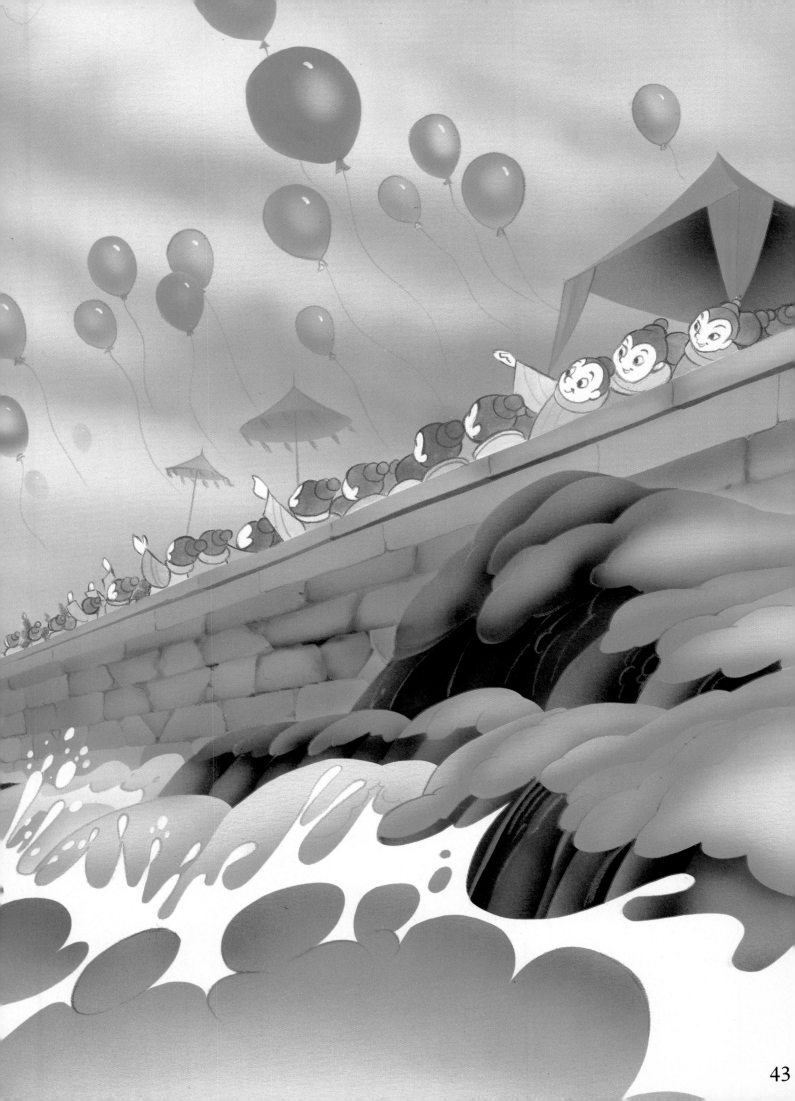

Two months later, Gulliver reached home. He visited the King to tell him about his wonderful journey and the friends he'd made. The King could hardly believe in an empire of six-inch people, but Gulliver produced a tiny horse and carriage to prove his story.

The King was very happy to learn of these new neighbors. He sent an ambassador to Lilliput at once. The large nation and the small one formed an alliance and enjoyed a prosperous friendship—all thanks to Gulliver's travels.